# ACTING ON

## and

## other short stories

by

Ian Mallendar
Joan Stanley
Mike Stanley
Lynda Wakeling
and
Pam Weaver

Red'n'Ritten Ltd.

Published by Red'n'Ritten Ltd, 17 Kings Barn Lane,
Steyning, West Sussex BN44 3YR
© Red'n'Ritten Ltd. 2001

ISBN 1-904278-05-1
A CIP Catalogue record for this book is available from the British Library.

Printed by Apollo Press, Worthing, West Sussex.
Cover Artwork by Ned Woodman

# ACTING ON IMPULSE
## and
### other short stories

**Contents:**

# SIMPSON

by

Ian Mallender

We returned to England in 1994. There were the two of us, plus two cats, two dogs and two horses. There is no doubt, Simpson was the boss: that ginger cat, the youngest member of the family, ruled the roost. Perhaps he blamed me for his six months' stay in quarantine.

It was a catastrophic day and that blasted cat started it.

I nudged the refrigerator door closed with my knees and, as I backed away, I felt a furry tail under my bare foot. Of course, it was too late to un-tread, but I tried to make myself lighter by leaping into the air.

Simpson yowled and dug his claws into my ankle. I dropped the eggs from my right hand. As they exploded, one on each side, he hissed and turned in retaliation against this new threat. My heart went out to him. I bent down to offer comfort, forgetting the bottle of milk, clutched tightly under my left elbow, to free my left hand for the butter dish.

As milk poured all over him Simpson decided he had suffered enough indignity. He scampered from the kitchen. A trail of milk and egg stretched across the hall carpet and into the bedroom where he jumped up on the bed, snarling and hissing, prepared to defend himself to the death. As I backed away he started cleaning himself to restore his self-esteem.

The smoke alarm in the hall let out an ear-splitting PEEP – PEEP – PEEP. Rushing back to the kitchen to find smoke pouring from the toaster, I skidded on the mixture of raw egg and milk. Both feet shot from under me, my dressing gown flared behind me, and I landed with a splash on my bare bum in the gooey mess.

As I lay there looking up at the cloud of smoke spreading across the ceiling, the smoke alarm's insistent PEEP-ing continued to penetrate my brain. I wished I had just stayed in bed.

Simpson came to investigate the noise and sat looking directly at me with a big, satisfied grin on his face. I took a swipe at him and slalomed across the floor.

The kettle decided this would be a good time to demand attention, its whistle joined in strident discord with the smoke alarm. I closed my eyes and put my hands over my ears; perhaps I would wake up later to find it had all been a terrible nightmare.

"What the devil is going on?"

I opened my eyes to find Tricia staring in amazement at me wallowing on the kitchen floor.

"It was that damned cat," I replied, rolling onto my hands and knees and making my way towards the doormat, where I hoped to get some purchase.

"Cover yourself," she shouted, as my crawling exposed my less attractive features. "You look like a blue-arsed baboon," she yelled above the pandemonium, "and stop that noise – and turn off the toaster before you burn the place down."

Reaching the mat, I grabbed the door handle and pulled myself upright. Holding onto the sink unit, I slid my way to the toaster, unplugged it, threw it in the sink and turned on the cold tap. I then skated to the stove and turned off the ring. The whistle slowly decayed through the octaves like the dying tones of a wartime air raid siren.

Pushing a stool into the hall I closed the kitchen door to stop the smoke emerging. I found the morning paper, and standing on the stool, frantically waved at the smoke alarm until it finally ceased. An eerie silence descended in the wake of screaming chaos.

"You've trampled goo all over the carpet," Tricia announced, looking up at me, as I towered above her, paper aloft, like some amateur portrayal of the Statue of Liberty. Beside her sat Simpson, looking from one to the other, encouraging her to give me hell.

We glared at each other, both madder than hell this early in the morning. "Stop bitching, woman, and start bailing."

My dressing gown fell open and her glare turned into a suppressed grin, before she finally exploded with laughter at the ridiculous sight before her. "Go and take a shower while I clear up and get breakfast."

I descended from my lofty position and stalked off to the bathroom with as much dignity as I could muster. Simpson sat and watched – gloating.

I was still uptight as I drove to work, fifteen minutes late, in drizzling rain and heavy traffic that got slower and slower. I decided to get off the main road and cut through the back streets.

Spotting a small gap in the oncoming traffic I checked the wing mirror and pulled out, indicating a right turn. Accelerating, I quickly glanced in the rear view mirror for cops and started an illegal U turn. Simpson!

Simpson was sitting on the shelf in the back window, one leg straight up in the air, calmly licking the place his testicles had once occupied.

I yelled, looked again, misjudged traffic, skidded, hit the curb, blew a tyre, stalled the engine and came to a halt, spread-eagled across two lanes.

Horns blasted all around and tyres screeched, while Simpson just hung on tight and glared at me accusingly, as if I had done it just to shake him up.

There was a crunch and a jolt as a lorry ploughed into the rear corner of my car, which upset Simpson still more. He turned and hissed through the window at the large driver, who was climbing down from his cab and approaching with menacing gait. I pushed the central locking button and looked straight ahead, hoping he would go away and wondering what else could go wrong.

Being unable to drive away because of the flat tyre, I thought I should at least try to get to the side of the road and restarted the engine.

The lorry driver was now joined by a growing mob. They surrounded the car making it impossible to move even a few yards to clear the road. Traffic was halted in both directions and I provided entertainment for a large audience, each vying with the next for the most original combinations of rude comments. Mobile phones were produced and calls made to say they would be late because some stupid nerd had blocked the road.

Remaining inside the locked car, I watched as the lorry driver began directing traffic around the mess. He was obviously prepared to wait as long as necessary to get at me.

I breathed a sigh of relief when a siren and a flashing light announced the arrival of the police; at least I wouldn't get lynched.

I emerged when the officer requested. He took my details, amid much shouting from the crowd.

"He should be in the nut house."

"Crazy blighter."

"Check his breath," were among the mildest comments.

The policeman finally asked me what happened. He gave me a strange look when I said "It was that damned cat."

No one had seen a cat. We searched, but Simpson was nowhere to be found.

"You'd better come along with me, sir," said the cop, leading me away.

I arrived home in a taxi that evening. "The car's in dock," I confessed to Tricia. "I had an accident," was all I was prepared to admit, having spent the entire day waiting around the police station and the garage, where the car had been towed.

She fussed a bit. Asked if I was hurt? If anyone was hurt? How it happened? I was monosyllabic in response, until she realised that I was not going to talk about it.

Then she changed the subject. "Simpson has been out all day," somewhat concerned, "I hope he's all right."

We had some food and watched TV in silence, before I went to bed, thankful that the day was over. I dreamt of Simpson, of all the things I would do to him.

I was awakened by a noise at the bedroom window. Burglars, I thought. In the darkness I slipped quietly out of bed, picked up a heavy shoe, tiptoed toward the window and whipped back the curtains to catch the intruder. No one was there.

I turned on the light and examined the windows. They were closed, except for a small one at the top to give a little fresh air. I drew the curtains again and turned to get back into bed.

There he was: curled up on top of the bed, tired after his long walk. He looked at me out of one eye. I reached out to grab him, to hurl him back out of the window, but he rolled onto his back and played cute, smiling at me and pawing the air with one paw.

I knew, from watching David Attenborough on TV, that this was the kind of submissive gesture that lions in the wild make when they are defeated by a superior. I had finally won the battle.

At last Simpson recognised me as the dominant being. From now on he would be no trouble.

I got back into bed and turned out the light. Simpson curled up beside me and began purring loudly. When I was fast asleep, secure in our new found relationship, he began bouncing up and down on my chest and clawing my shoulder. Blurry eyed, I turned on the light.

Simpson shot towards the door where he sat looking at me, demanding that I get out of bed and open it for him. I helped him along with my foot.

End

# THIRTY SOMETHING

by

Lynda Wakeling

I really love Tuesdays. I work four days a week at the local primary school, but on Tuesday I do what I like, or that's the theory.

Eight forty five in the morning is the best time; everyone has left the house by then. The kids have gone to school, James to work, even the dog has settled back into her basket after her early morning walk. Everywhere is peaceful; I can sit at the kitchen table and really enjoy my second cup of coffee.

As I sat savouring the aroma of the granules at the bottom of my cup, I heard the plop of post hitting the mat in the hall. I had hoped for a letter from my sister today. It would have been a nice excuse to linger a bit longer, before getting stuck into the washing up.

I got up and opened the door to the hall. Oh, no! There it sat, just where it landed: a large pink envelope bearing my name. Why did it have to come today? It's not my birthday today.

I did not open it. It could wait on the hall table until tomorrow.

Of course, I knew it's from Mum and Dad; Mum makes sure she posts our cards in plenty of time. She says it's no use at all if cards arrive late. I didn't want it today. Today, I wanted to hold back the encroaching years.

Why do you think I'm punishing myself with exercise I've loathed doing since I was at secondary school?

And anyway, I can picture what's sitting there waiting for me inside that hideously bright envelope: a beautiful picture of hearts and flowers and amongst the blooms that horrible number.

Four is such an ugly number. Hard and angular. And on my card that four will be followed by an ugly, fat zero. Anyway, today I am still only thirty something. Thirty-nine to be precise. Thirty-nine sounds right, somehow. It sounds as though you could still be vaguely interesting, lively minded and even desirable.

Three is such a sexy number, all voluptuous curves – a bit like me, really. And nine doesn't look too bad either. But forty! Forty is simply hideous. Forty is old and stuffy and past giving a second glance to. Forty is a saggy bottom and grey hair and I don't want to be forty.

I was looking at myself in the long bedroom mirror last night. Gravity certainly seems to be taking control of my hindquarters. So I considered going for a swim at the local pool today, or even doing some jogging.

James said, last week, that he loves the little streak of grey hair just to the left of my parting. I hate it. Heaven knows I would never have the whole lot dyed red like my friend, Sue. But I decided that some gentle highlights would give me a lift.

I took the plunge – not literally, I changed my mind about going swimming. I telephoned that new, upmarket hair salon that has just opened in town.

"Yes," they said, "our Styling Director, Jason, can fit you in for a re-style at noon. Due," they pointed out, "to a most unexpected cancellation. Usually you have to book weeks in advance to get Jason."

I felt stupidly humble and ridiculously grateful that the great god Jason was able to take me in hand personally.

At the salon, I nervously produced a picture that I'd cut from a magazine.

"No, I can't possibly reproduce that style with hair this texture," he said, as he fingered strands of my, then, shoulder-length brown bob. I felt embarrassed and apologetic for the condition of my hair, which I really hadn't thought was too bad before I stepped into the salon.

"Trust me," Jason said and he told me I needed a lot of weight taken away from my face; that my style was very seventies and the whole thing was dragging me down.

Gravity prevailing, again. He began to snip away; in fact, I thought he was never going to stop.

"This is going to be so easy for you to style," he said. I gawped at my reflection in the mirror. 'Help!' I was unable to speak. 'I'm almost bald. What one earth will James say?'

I handed over an excessive amount of cash to the trendy young thing at the reception desk.

"Looks great," she told me. I was too much of a coward to disagree.

It's probably going to take three months to grow my hair back into some sort of order. Meanwhile, what am I going to do? Wear a paper bag over my head?

I cried as I closed the front door behind me. I peered into the hall mirror, trying to avoid looking at that leering cerise envelope on the table. I just want to look 'with it', modern, stylish, thirty-nine! Now I look like an upturned lavatory brush.

Surely, my appearance should reflect me, my self-image, but a stranger is staring back at me. A stranger who looks hard and angular. Just like that bloody number forty.

End

# BUBBLE TENNIS

by

Pam Weaver

The doors of the 5.45 p.m. tube train rumbled shut and it moved into the tunnel.

"Shall I?"

"Go on, then."

The schoolgirls sitting opposite Kirstie giggled all the time. No one else spoke or even smiled. After the friendliness of her home town, Kirstie wondered if she'd ever get used to this cool southern reserve.

The opportunity to work as trouble-shooter in the London office for six months had come as a complete surprise. It had been timely, too; her break-up with Jason had left her bruised and hurt.

"It'll do you good. You deserve a new start and you'll soon make friends." Mam had tried to be sympathetic.

Kirstie sighed. She had made one or two friends, including Sophie and Cathy from the aerobics class, but they were both attached.

"What you need is a new man. Go clubbing in the West End."

"It's the only way to meet a bloke."

But Kirstie wasn't the night-clubbing type, especially not on her own.

One of the girls rummaged inside her school bag and produced a small yellow tube of something and a long straw. Kirstie watched as she carefully removed the cap from the tube. Giggling and nudging her friend, the girl squeezed a small blob of glue-like substance onto the end of the straw. A sickly odour filled the compartment. Kirstie looked at the other passengers, but there was no reaction.

The girl replaced the cap and put the tube back into her bag. But instead of sniffing the glue, as Kirstie expected, she put the clean end of the straw into her mouth and began to blow.

A bubble appeared. Small at first, but it grew larger with every breath. When it was about the size of a football, the girl flicked her wrist and the bubble floated free. Almost at once, it rose gracefully towards the ceiling and stopped. Then it began an equally dignified descent. Kirstie smiled as the two girls began an impromptu tennis match.

The train slowed to a halt and remained motionless. People stopped talking. The only sound in the carriage was a loud mechanical knocking … something to do with the engine?

No one seemed to be bothered by it. Being stuck in the darkened tunnel between stations was an everyday occurrence.

The train gave a sudden lurch. Everybody in the carriage watched the bubble begin to float dangerously near the floor. Instinctively, Kirstie leapt to her feet and hit the bubble back into the air. She looked around. Every eye was upon her.

Oh, Lord, why on earth had she done that? She frowned, wishing the floor would open up and swallow her. For the first time in years, she felt her face flame with embarrassment.

There was a sudden movement in the far corner as a man, dressed in flowing African robes, screwed his copy of The Times recklessly in one hand and made a superb dive, almost to the floor, to hit the bubble back to her. But before it reached her again, a city gent sitting three seats away, jumped to his feet. "Good shot!" he cried as he cuffed the bubble back along the carriage.

Kirstie couldn't believe her eyes. A spotty-faced teenager with a nose ring hit the bubble towards a strap-hanging Vicar. The Vicar lobbed a brilliant shot back up the carriage towards a workman, but before the bubble reached him, a nurse launched herself between them and hit it back to Kirstie.

The whole train had suddenly become an army of bubble patters.

A tall man, athletic and good looking, fell against Kirstie as she reached for the bubble. "Sorry, luv," his accent gave him away immediately.

"You're from up North!"

He laughed. "And so are you. Are you on holiday?"

It was good to hear his beautiful accent, but it made Kirstie feel even more homesick. "I work here."

Another hand came between them and lifted the bubble back down the carriage. He took the opportunity to stand next to her. "I've only just moved down here. Takes a bit of getting used to after the green, green grass of home."

Kirstie remembered the panoramic views of home and laughed. "They think it's all docks and dereliction up north, don't they?"

The bubble sailed between them again, but Kirstie let it go.

"I'm Greg."

"Kirstie."

"Out of the way!" The nurse gave the bubble a Wimbledon style volley back towards the African.

Greg held out his hand. "Pleased to meet you, Kirstie."

As their fellow passengers pushed and jostled Kirstie had difficulty keeping her balance. "Can you believe this?"

Smiling, he shook his head.

"Go on, go on!" The schoolgirls waved their arms in the air, "Hit it!"

"Oh no, I missed ..."

The train lurched again and moved on through the black tunnel. As it gathered speed, the passengers began to lose interest in the bubble. Smiling and nodding, they sat down in their seats or went back to strap-hanging.

Eventually, someone hit the bubble onto the ceiling where it stuck.

"For one brief moment, the whole world went bananas."

Greg's eyes twinkled. "Great, wasn't it?"

Kirstie nodded and turned to face the doors. Pity she'd never see him again. He looked nice.

The carriage burst through the darkness into the glaring lights of the station. As soon as the train stopped, the doors slid open and Kirstie stepped onto the platform.

"Hey Kirstie ..." She spun round. Greg was still behind her, a sports bag thrown carelessly over one shoulder. "I just wondered ... are you into sport?"

"Aerobics and swimming."

Greg pulled a face. "I'm more your weights and badminton man. But perhaps we could meet up afterwards for a coffee?"

"I'd love to."

"And maybe," he added, "we'll discover a sport we'd both enjoy."

Kirstie gave him a wry smile, "Well … we both know we're pretty good at bubble tennis."

End

# SIXTH SENSE

by

Pam Weaver

"Hi, Cathy. This is Chad ..."

Jill turned towards the answering machine. Chad? Who on earth was Chad?

Bonnie let out a little bark.

"I'm coming to England," Chad went on. "Cathy, Honey, I gotta see you again. The usual place, OK? Call me back."

Jill's romantic streak soared. Poor Chad ... He sounded so in love and he was obviously excited. But he'd dialled the wrong number and got through to her answering machine instead of Cathy's.

Jill sighed; she'd have to ring back and explain. She reached for the receiver to make a call back, but there was a clink and a voice on the tape said, "Jill, it's Mum. We're having roast lamb for lunch. Can you bring me some rosemary and mint from the garden? Byeee."

No point in dialling 1471 now. Jill rewound the tape.

"Hi, Cathy. This is Chad ..."

Jill could feel Bonnie's tail thumping against her leg. She reached down to pat her. "He sounds really nice, doesn't he? Lucky old Cathy. I hope he rings again."

Lunch was fabulous, but then Mum always produced perfect Sunday roasts. Jill's rosemary and mint set the lamb off wonderfully well; the family were impressed with her newly started herb garden.

Dad chuckled, "Your sense of smell must be top notch."

Her brother Don was home from university for the weekend with Su, his new girlfriend. He steered Jill into the big armchair so that he and Su could cuddle up on the sofa.

"How are you managing in your new flat?" Don asked, when he and Su came up for air.

"Fine."

"And the job?"

"Couldn't be better."

Su was curious, "What do you do?"

"I'm a translator."

"You must have very good hearing."

"She has." Don was proud of his sister's achievement.

Normally Jill would have been delighted with the compliment, but her thoughts kept drifting back to Chad. He'd go to meet Cathy at the usual place, and she'd let him down ... or so it would seem ...

"You're miles away," Don observed. "What is it, a man?"

Jill was tempted to tell them, but how could she tell them she fancied a man she'd never even met?

The following Sunday, she and Bonnie went to the park. The weather was warm and Bonnie enjoyed her times off the lead. Jill always sat on the bench next to the rose garden where she could revel in a good book, but it was hard to concentrate.

They'd just returned; when Jill pressed the play button on her phone she heard his voice again: "Hi, Cathy. It's Chad again ..."

Bonnie jumped up and put her paws on the hall table. Her sudden movement almost made Jill stumble.

"Bonnie!"

"I'll arrive at noon on Friday," Chad went on. "I hope you got my last message. I'll meet you at Hunters, 10.30 on Saturday, OK?"

There were no other messages, so Jill dialled 1471.

"You were called today at 11.05. The caller withheld their number."

Oh, no! Chad seemed fated. Hunters ... where was that? She'd ask her father. After all, Dad was a taxi driver – a mine of information.

This Sunday's roast was pork and, with Jill's basil, it was a marriage made in heaven. Half way through the meal, she broached the subject of Hunters.

21

Dad pondered, "I'm sure I should know it, but I just can't place it."

"It's that little café next to the library," Mum reminded him.

Jill told them about Chad. "I've decided to go there and meet him myself."

"But he's never set eyes on you," Dad protested. "How will you know it's him?"

"I shall know him the minute he opens his mouth," Jill smiled.

She arrived at Hunters at 10.15. And she was nervous. There were a few tables outside on the pavement. Jill sat outside to enjoy the sunshine. The café was popular; its warm friendly atmosphere was filled with the murmur of voices.

He came at 10.25. Jill heard him talking to the waitress; his velvety accent gave him away at once.

"I'll order in a moment," he was saying. "Right now, I'm waiting for somebody."

Jill approached him nervously. "Excuse me, are you Chad?"

"Sure ... I'm sorry, but do I know you?"

Jill could feel her face burning. Her legs went to jelly. She took a deep breath. "We've actually never met, but you've been leaving messages on my answer machine ..."

As soon as he checked his address book he realised his mistake. "I was one digit out." Jill lent him her mobile; he rang Cathy and arranged to meet her later on.

When the waitress came back for his order Jill stood up to leave.

"No, no," Chad protested, "let me buy you a coffee … it's the least I can do." So, they spent the rest of the morning in the café. One coffee led to another and, before long, Jill was eating lunch, too.

Chad told her he was working for an aid agency, helping to set up health clinics in third world countries. "I love it," he enthused, "and Cathy first talked me into it."

"How long have you been going out together?" The question was out before Jill could stop herself.

Chad chuckled. "We're not … Cathy is the fund-raiser for the British end of the organisation."

"I see …" Jill's heart was thumping.

"And she's seventy four if she's a day."

Jill laughed aloud. Why was she feeling so light hearted?

"You look so beautiful when you smile," he said suddenly.

Jill felt herself blush again. Bonnie nuzzled against her. "And what about you?"

"Be my guest."

Jill leaned forward. He smelled of lemon with a hint of almond. She reached out her hand and let her fingers wander all over his face. Her sixth sense was right. He was every bit as gorgeous as he sounded.

End

# ACTING ON IMPULSE

by

Pam Weaver

Liz put the reference book down. She was right. This proved it. "Miniatures by Lavina Tearlink, sixteenth century. Eagerly sought for their scarcity."

"Well?" Miss Duncan was staring at her expectantly. "Will you buy it?"

"I'd love to," Liz began, "but you'd get a far better price at auction."

The reply was clipped: "I need the cash now."

"It's beautiful quality, Miss Duncan." Liz turned the book around so that the old lady could see for herself. "Read what it says. I really must advise ..."

"Elizabeth ..." Miss Duncan didn't even look down at the page. "I want to sell this miniature to you. Will you take it or not?"

Liz shook her head apologetically. "The maximum I can offer is £5,000."

"Done!"

If Liz hadn't trusted Miss Duncan so implicitly, she would have been suspicious of her eagerness to sell. She'd known the old lady for years.

Liz had always prided herself that she had given Miss Duncan fair prices, although often Liz's heart ruled her head. "I'll get a banker's draft by tomorrow," Liz told her.

Twenty-four hours later, the miniature lay in the office safe.

"I hope it's what I think it is." She couldn't bring herself to tell her husband how much she had paid for it.

When he saw it, Mike's comment was comprehensive. "It's gross."

Until Liz had the miniature valued, life was unbearable. One minute she imagined selling an imitation for £50, the next she was planning a world cruise with the auction money she got from the genuine article.

"If it does turn out to be worth a lot of money, I want us to offer Miss Duncan a bit more."

Mike laughed. "You're mad. We'll never get rich at this rate."

"I prefer to be fair."

"And here's me thinking we were trying to make a living."

"Not if it means diddling old ladies."

Mike kissed her cheek. "I take it all back, you're not mad, you're completely nuts."

Tony Paton, the valuer, sounded enthusiastic. "I'm not sure about its authenticity, but I've got an American buyer who's interested in miniatures. He'll offer anything up to £5,000. I honestly don't think you'll get any more, not even at auction. Are you still selling?"

Liz swallowed hard. "Yes, yes of course."

Damn! She'd get exactly what she'd paid for it. It was disappointing, but at least she hadn't made a loss.

When Mike realised the risk she'd taken, he was livid. "You're always acting on impulse, you sentimental idiot! You could have lost us our credibility and damaged the business."

"It could have been a lot worse," she mumbled defiantly.

Two days later, it was. The phone rang. It was Paton: "My report is in the post. It's a fake."

"It can't be!" Liz protested wildly. "The quality of the paint ... the subject ..."

"We did all the tests, the blue background is definitely modern and the woman's face looks yellow under ultra-violet light. If it was sixteenth century, the face would have been lead white. I hope you didn't part with any money."

The phone went dead. Paton smiled. His son watched him with a puzzled expression. "Isn't it a bit of a gamble to let it go?"

"Leave her a couple of days to face that husband of hers, and she'll be only too glad to sell it to me for a song."

"What then?"

"Then my boy, we'll be rich. There's only a dozen or so of those miniatures left. It's got to be worth fifty grand of anyone's money."

Liz, her hand still on the receiver, stared into space. Inside she was shaking, £5,000 for a worthless miniature.

She'd have to get the money back. Mike would go ballistic.

Could she cancel the banker's order? Did Miss Duncan realise it was a fake?

She set off at once for 81, Bulkington Avenue, the miniature at the bottom of her handbag. The house looked empty, a 'For Sale' board leaned drunkenly over the fence. In the road outside, the council workmen were loading boxes into a dustcart.

Liz knocked fiercely on the door, but there was no reply. Presently a woman's head appeared over the fence. "If you're looking for Miss Duncan, she's gone."

Liz felt her mouth go dry. "Gone? Gone where?"

"I think it was Australia, she wanted to spend her last days with her sister."

"Last days?" Liz knew she was sounding ridiculous.

"It's very sad," the neighbour went on. "The cancer had really taken hold. She hasn't got long to live." The woman studied her face carefully and added, "Here, are you called Liz?" Liz nodded stiffly.

"I've got a letter for you." And a few minutes later, she handed Liz a small pink envelope.

Stuffing it into her pocket, Liz turned to go, muttering bitterly to herself. "I bet she knew it was worthless. I've been had, and by the oldest trick in the book."

As she walked past the dustcart, Liz had a strong impulse to chuck the miniature inside and watch it disappear under the crusher.

Back home, she spread the letter on her lap. Whatever was she going to tell Mike? It would take them ages to pay off £5,000.

Through her tears, Liz tried to focus on the words.

*Dear Liz,'* Miss Duncan wrote, *'Thank you for giving me the money I needed. I expect by now you've discovered the woman in the miniature is Mary Tudor. I wanted you to have it anyway. Sotheby's say it's worth at least £80,000. I've left it to you in my will. Sell it and be happy.'*

Liz felt her stomach churn. Thank goodness, this was the one time she hadn't acted on impulse.
End

# A FITTING TALE

by

Joan Stanley

My grandmother had all the same lumps and bumps as me and yet she looked gorgeous, a real beauty. Born to a life in domestic service, she had no fancy budget, but she certainly gained ideas on how to dress well from her employer; her clothes were fitted to enhance the good bits and camouflage the rest.

At the turn of the last century the designers had the advantage of knowing that every woman was prepared to suffer heavy corsetry. These days most of us prefer to let it all hang out with disastrous results.

We can't all be Scarlet O'Hara's with eighteen-inch waists. In those days, even the old dowagers, with their twenty-eight or even thirty-eight-inch middles, looked as though they enjoyed their clothes, whereas, for me, it has always been an exercise in damage limitation.

Like most of my sex, I do not want to make my own clothes; I have better things to do with my time and I'm not much good at dressmaking. But I really am fed up with what the High Street has to offer. It is a sad day when any woman has to admit that she has returned home, from a shopping spree, empty handed for want of temptation.

Today's creations are expected to fit, if that is the right word, all shapes and sizes. The tubes, made in clingy materials, may be OK for the straight up and down size eights. They do nothing for us that have excess pounds in all the wrong places. Do designers go out of their way to cause maximum embarrassment and depression?

I persuaded my husband to accompany me to London to find a winter coat. When I set out that morning I deliberately wore my tracksuit legs and stretched hand-knitted jumper. I had no choice about the coat, it was the only one I had – a man's waterproof jacket from the agricultural supplier.

Here I was, expecting to pay serious money for something more elegant and only last week I had congratulated myself for replacing the defunct zip with a piece of Velcro, costing forty p. I wanted a completely new look. I knew what I was looking for; clothes that fitted.

We traipsed up and down Regent Street and Oxford Street. Young petites in thousand pound coats looked happily at their images in shop mirrors. Even at that price I found nothing.

Shopping is not my favourite activity. Distant memories of attentive assistants still teased me. I resented being left to pick my way through over-packed racks. Bending over, nose in the air, I struggled to find and read garment labels through the lower half of my varifocals.

Then, when I thought I had found something that could possibly fit, I was pointed to a telephone kiosk.

Fed up with the crowds, and lack of customer care, I felt as though the retail clothing industry had rendered me irrelevant. All I wanted was something that fitted, felt comfortable and didn't make me look like a sack of spuds with a string tied round the middle.

We decided to find a tailor, who made clothes for women, and find out how much he would charge.

Leaving Regent Street for her parallel sister, we strolled down Saville Row looking for inspiration. One shop had an outdated woman's costume bashfully in view. It did not inspire confidence. I went in to make enquiries, to find that the man who dealt with women was out. I thought it was just as well.

Further down the street sale signs dominated the view. The 'On Her Majesty's Service' sign was a bit daunting, but by now I was desperate. My husband fell in ten paces behind; I could sense sweat breaking out all over his wallet.

Peering into the entrance I saw a dress on a dummy, it was short and dumpy. I took heart. They obviously had realistic expectations of their customers' needs. Maybe they could cope with tall and plump, as well. I took a deep breath, plucked up courage and entered.

The look on the immaculate receptionist's face alone was worth the enquiry. I got the feeling that she didn't think we were of the same species. She was undoubtedly right. As usual there were no prices on show. I had no idea what to expect. Hundreds? Thousands? There was only one way to find out. "Good morning."

A raised feminine eyebrow responded to my greeting.

A tall young man stepped forward, complete with beaming smile. "Good morning. Can I help you?"

I did not know to whom I should direct my enquiry. I found myself alternating between the two, glancing first at one and then the other.

It soon became apparent that the young gentleman was not going to let any snobbery get in the way of a potential sale.

"I don't know if I'm in the right place. I have no idea what you charge or if I can begin to afford it."

Both eyebrows disappeared into the lady's well-styled hairline.

Idiot, I rebuked myself. If you have to ask the price you can take it for granted that you can't afford it.

"Please follow me. My name is Nicholas."

My husband and I were ushered into a room and shown a rack of garments left at the end of their sale. The first thing that caught my eye was a size flag: size 22. Too big - hope blossomed. They had three trouser suits in my nominal size.

We were taken upstairs to a lounge. My husband sighed with relief as he settled himself into one of the enormous settees. I was shown to a screened off area with enough room to swing a modest cat, and discreetly left to try on one suit after the other. Two of the outfits did not begin to stretch round my girth or down to my wrists and ankles.

I tried on the third jacket. A patterned biscuit colour, not the most exciting material you have ever seen, but it fitted. Not just here and there, it looked as if it had been made for me. Even more than that, all the lumps and bumps had disappeared. Even Nicholas could not hide his surprise. The trousers were a squeeze. With the waist done up I looked pregnant, they needed to be several inches bigger and the legs were too short.

"Don't worry. Leave it all to our tailor, he is extremely good."

"What's the bad news?"

"We charge by the hour."

"How much?"

The figure quoted shocked me. "That's great. It's less than I pay to get my car fixed."

"I suppose if you look at it like that it's not so bad."

"He's going to have to be a miracle worker to fit these trousers." I took them off and examined the seams and darts, maybe, just maybe … The waistband would have to be faked.

Nicholas told me about a young lady who had returned with clothes she had inherited from her grandmother and how they had been remade to suit her. "You should treat our clothes like heirlooms. Your daughter will be able to have them remade in later years."

We got chatting, as you do, and I discovered that Nicholas lived quite near us. Extremely polite, he was not at all stuck up. His naturally relaxed manner, as we gossiped, made what could have been a traumatic experience a real treat.

As I removed the trousers I looked down at my socks, complete with very neat darns. That did nothing to take away the embarrassment I felt. Nicholas was obviously very proud of the standard of service and the quality of garments he sold.

"You can tell that I will look after my clothes from my socks."

He didn't bat an eyelid.

Standing in the jacket, fortunately a long one, less than glamorous underwear and my husband's cast off hosiery, my excess inches were painfully obvious. How I wished I were size twelve again.

Alan arrived promptly, a neat slim man with the confidence of one who has spent many years perfecting his craft. Cocking his head to one side, he viewed the problem from every angle. Even he seemed a bit taken aback.

Then he popped a pin in here and another in there. His professional skill was being challenged, but his determination to prove that the age of miracles was not yet over was evident.

I told Nicholas about our disastrous attempts to find a coat; he excused himself and in two minutes returned with a moss green double breasted long jacket and scarf.

"This is in the sale. I think it might suit you."

I had never felt such soft material. I tried it on. It felt like a baby's cobweb shawl. It transformed my whole appearance. Then I lifted my hands and the wretched sleeves walked up my arms.

"You see my problem, Nicholas. It's always the same. I love this coat, it's so warm and so lightweight. Usually jacket sleeves go halfway up to my elbows when I do that."

"Gosh, that's a shame."

He was genuinely disappointed for me. "There is no extra material hidden in the lining, it's a double thickness soft wool.

"Look at this, Alan." I extended my monkey arms to demonstrate the problem to the tailor.

"What a pity, it looks so good on you. A perfect fit on the shoulders ..."

Nicholas and Alan tried unsuccessfully to think of ways to obtain more material. He named the stuff; I don't remember what it's called.

This time it was my turn to demonstrate a bit of expertise. "Couldn't you take some material off the scarf and add some cuffs."

"Would you mind? We can certainly do that." Alan pulled a face, "The bad news is that this material is sewn by hand."

By now I was past caring, I just knew that this coat was the nearest thing to fitting perfection I had had on my back in living memory, and Alan was going to be the one to redesign the sleeves.

"How much?"

Nicholas worked out the price of the garments and Alan estimated the alteration costs. Then came the moment of truth. I could have hugged them both; the total, with the suit, was much less than I expected to pay for a coat alone.

My feet are in direct proportion to the rest of me. Nicholas recommended a good shoe shop. They, too, had a sale on. I found a beautiful pair of lamb's skin shoes and insisted my husband bought himself some new shoes, too.

In the train home we reviewed the day. We both felt it would go down in history as a great success.

The next day my husband brought home a £4.50 tee shirt with a panda printed on it. That was good, too. For a week or so I had to take some stick from the family as their answer to the "pretty woman", I can live with that.

I chose to go back and collect my clothes. Not only had Alan made the trousers big enough, but there was a bit of space to spare. I still have not worked out how he managed to revamp the waistband without it showing.

Since then I have received an invitation to go and see their Spring and Summer Collection. Nicholas is not optimistic that I shall find the summer frock I'm looking for, but he assures me that I shall enjoy the occasion.

All I need is a new wardrobe to store my new collection. Oh yes, I shall be going back. I might be a country yokel who spends most of my time slouching around in tracksuits and tee shirts, but, given half an excuse, I shall now be pleased to dress up.

You see, I like to wear hats, but there is no way in which I can wear a nice hat with a waterproof farming jacket. I am fed up to the back teeth with having to wear men's clothes; even my latest jumper was bought in the men's department in M&S. Men's tracksuit bottoms, jumpers, jackets, shirts … it's been the only way in which I can get garments with long enough legs and sleeves.

Have I gone back in time to a century when shop assistants really could have pride in helping their customers choose what is right for them? I do hope so. Although in my wildest dreams I could not call Nicholas a shop assistant. I wonder what his job title really is? From now on shopping is going to be an experience, not torture to be endured.

Not only do I expect to look a lot better, but it has given me an incentive to attack my keyboard with renewed vigour, for I intend to earn myself enough money to afford a completely new wardrobe and fill it with clothes that fit and give me pleasure, not shame, to wear.

How much did I spend? I'm not telling. Suffice to say I went to London with the intention of committing actual bodily harm to my flexible friend and in the event it was only mildly abused.
End

# I'VE GOT A LITTLE SHOP

by

Joan Stanley

Hello, you on holiday, too? It's real nice 'ere, i'n't it? I love the sea. I could sit 'ere all day watching the kiddies paddling and making sandcastles. I only went to the seaside once when I was a tot, on a Sunday School Outing.

Now I come whenever I can. It's not often I get time off. A real treat this is. I work all the hours God sends. Never have time to put me feet up, in the normal way.

You see, I've got a little shop. I'm very fond of my little shop. In fact, you could say I love my little shop.

I put all the packets on the shelves, and tins, of course, in neat rows like soldiers. All their faces, silly me, all their labels lined up, all neat and tidy like. Look a real treat they do.

The apples are polished. The pears stood up on their fat bums, beg your pardon, bottoms. The bananas can get a bit contrary. They never want to lie down the way I like 'em to. Real difficult they can be. I get 'em just right and they go and get 'emselves sold or go brown and squashy and I have to take 'em all off again.

41

There's a real art in stacking sugar. If you don't pat 'em down firmly and put 'em in their place, they all tumble down. And do they make a mess when those bags split? I'll say so. Gritty stuff gets everywhere.

'Ave you ever walked on sugar? It's dreadful stuff. 'Ave you over, as soon as not. Like trying to walk on marbles. And just when you think you're ok, it crunches under your feet and makes you feel all nervous.

Funny that. Sugar's supposed to be good for the nerves.

I suppose I like the delicatessen customers best. The cold counter food wouldn't keep long, anyway, so I may as well sell it.

I love it when the factory boys turn up and queue for their sandwiches. Chicken's their favourite. They all go for my freshly cooked, free-range chicken.

And why not? It's very good. Even if I do say it myself, as shouldn't.

"Are you a leg or breast man?" I say.

Oh, dear me. I love to see those lads colour up. It gets 'em every time. And their mates rag 'em something wicked. The whole shop laughs at the one in front, as he goes from virgin pink to beetroot red. I keep a dead straight face.

Funny that, I've never been good at poker.

Speaking of beetroot, it reminds me of my husband. I dropped a bottle, a full bottle mind, of whisky. Was he furious! He went on and on about the mess and of course he wasn't bothered about the mess at all.

I'm not sure to this day whether it was the waste of drink or the waste of money; he likes a little drink, does my old man.

Well, as I was saying, he went on something rotten about this blooming whisky and what does he go and do? He drops a jar of beetroot.

Now beetroot don't cost very much compared to whisky. But, oh, my Lor', you should have seen the place. You see the beetroot was on the shelf above the tea, custard, blancmange, and the neatly shaped packets I was telling you about. And this shelf was over the flour and sugar, which was laid out in a trough on the floor.

Well, the beetroot jar fell: crash - down on the tiled concrete floor. Exploded. And before you could say, "nuts", the whole section looked as though it 'ad got measles. Broken glass and little red spots of beetroot stained vinegar sprayed everywhere.

You may not believe it, but we 'ad to take pounds and pounds of stuff off the shelves. It cost far more than my bottle of whisky. I never let 'im forget it. I remind 'im of it, whenever he gets above 'imself.

Did you hear about the coal-man? Talking about getting above 'imself. He invited Mrs Willowby out. You know the snooty woman from The Crescent. He did. He actually 'ad the nerve to ask 'er to the theatre. I mean, what's the likes of 'im doing going to the theatre? Not only did he ask, but she went. She did.

And you'll never guess what they did afterwards, they …

Blast, the delivery-man's arrived. I've got loads of stuff coming in, lots of special offers. You wait 'til I get 'em unpacked. You'll love the new cakes.

What about the coal-man? I can't stop now I must get out back. That delivery–man is such a clumsy blighter. If I'm not there to stop 'im he'll wheel 'is trolleys all over my dahlias. I love my dahlias. I take a lot of trouble over 'em … I can't spend all day talking gardening. I must get on.

Why do you keep going on about the coal-man? Come in tomorrow and you can buy some of my new cakes while I tell you all about 'im and 'er from The Crescent. Must go. Bye for now.

End

# DO COMPUTERS IMPROVE A MAN'S IMAGE?

by

Mike Stanley

Age has been kind to Eric. Over the years, the number of grey hairs has increased and now he looks quite distinguished.

Eric is a mathematical modeller of high repute. He discovered how to accelerate nature's blanching process when he acquired a computer. Each year spent in dialogue with his electronic tormentor has been repaid with an increase in silver highlights. As the grey hairs multiplied so did his self-confidence. Now younger men seek his advice on how to improve their image.

The first box, called It, had been tamed and taught to communicate in Basic and Fortran. As their relationship developed, this dedicated boffin persuaded his computer to use a Supercalc4 spreadsheet. But It got possessive.

Having conquered It's temper tantrums, Eric decided that a byte of sibling rivalry would be a good idea. A second computer, Other, was duly installed. It took a bit of time to break Other in. Patience was eventually rewarded, and more silver threads appeared.

This new edition to the family was very flexible. But Other had a mind of its own and could be very manipulative. Soon, Eric was neglecting 4, having been persuaded to give his attention to Supercalc5.

This infidelity was to be the direct cause of many wrong decisions. However, help was at hand. Excel was encouraged to assert its authority and peace reigned once more.

Eric did not forget It. Faithful service should be recognised. After all, It did house a complete library of working programs, which were still useful. You may ask why he needed Other at all. One night, after a few beers, he confessed. Officially, it had been in the name of Progress. In reality, it had been for more grey hairs.

Other was bigger, faster and more complex. High stress levels were guaranteed. Computational Fluid Dynamic equations were soon line dancing up and down the VDU, enabling Eric to predict glass heat flow in three dimensions. His joy was orgasmic.

Other only died once. Expected to work on its first birthday, it sulked. An IBM para-computic was called in who soon eradicated the bug. Meanwhile, our greying friend slid along his desk to work on It. He needed to produce a report on Other's first death.

Other was pacified and continued to chunter away for hours at a time, processing Eric's computations.

In many ways Eric thinks this routine is unsuitable for a vertically thinking male, he feels that his laterally thinking female counterpart would manage the process better.

It decided not to work after the 31st December 1999. The company has decided to put It out to grass for faithful commitment to the science of mathematical modelling.

Timing is fortuitous. Eric's ego needs a boost. As a result of sitting in front of It for long hours, his waistline has increased in direct proportion to his grey hair count. Her-At-Home is worried that the increased weight will affect his health. She is talking about a physical fitness programme.

Another, his third box, has been ordered. The stress potential is exciting. All things being equal, his remaining black strands will be awarded the distinguished order of EPNS. Eric is hoping that Her-At-Home will be so much in awe of his silver crown that she will forget all about diets, exercise and heart disease.

What did you say? What has age got to do with it?

End

# JUNK

by

Joan Stanley

Linda sprayed the tabletop, liberally, with polish. Giving it a good rub, she admired herself in the shiny surface.

Her mother stormed into the dining room. "What on earth do you think you're doing? Have I taught you nothing?"

"Now what?" Linda poked her head out from under the old piece of furniture where she was systematically pulling her cloth to and fro over the legs and cross bars.

"Spray polish. What the hell do you think you are doing putting that rubbish on my old wood?"

"It's easy and it looks good."

"Your grandmother will turn over in her grave." Bet marched out of the room huffing and puffing while her daughter continued her labours.

Handing Linda a tin of beeswax wrapped in a clean yellow duster, the old woman insisted, "Use this. Not only are you determined to destroy my furniture with that modern muck, you're not using a proper cloth to do it with."

"Oh, Mum, you are impossible, anyone would think it was worth a fortune."

"It might be for all we know. Your Gran always used to say, 'Look after the old things and they will look after you on a rainy day.'"

"I think you've got your metaphors a bit mixed up, Mum."

"My what-aphors?"

"Anyway, I bet it's not worth half what she paid for it."

Bet's forefinger enforced her argument, "Don't you scoff young lady. There's many a collector made a fortune out of antiques."

"And there's many who have lost a packet."

Linda loved to wind her mother up. The supposed value of her junk was a sore subject. Bet rose to the bait. "Look at your Uncle Jim,"

"Must I? He isn't very good looking."

"Can't you ever take anything seriously?"

"Go on, then. What about Uncle Jim?"

"He's collected tins all his life and expects to retire on 'em."

"I think a bed would be more comfortable." Linda held her hands up in submission, warding off her mother's wrath. "OK, carry on."

"It's his hobby; he's had a lot of them since he was a boy and he says they'll be worth a mint by the time he's seventy."

"That's not a hobby, that's an obsession."

Linda dutifully picked up the pristine yellow duster and wiped it across the honeyed surface of the tinned wax.

"I suppose you'll have me keeping these polish tins next."

"There's no need to be sarcastic. Jim's got hundreds of tins. I've seen 'em, they've taken over his spare bedroom. They give him a lot of pleasure."

"If it's pleasure he wants he'd do better to throw the lot out and take in a nice young widow to keep him company."

"Linda!"

"Well, he would."


The wax polish took some working in and Linda was getting hot. "This is a lot harder work than the other stuff. Don't you think it's got a heady smell?"

"No I don't. It makes the place smell cared for and dignified."

"Dignified? Us? Do behave!"

"Behave, yourself. I know what's right. I was not put out to domestic service without learning a thing or two." Bet folded her arms, nestling them up under her ample bosom. Sticking her nose up in the air, "And if beeswax was good enough for their furniture it's good enough for mine."

Linda gave up. This was an argument she knew, from long experience, she hadn't got a hope of winning. She tried a different tack, "Anyway, he buys most of his tins from the local junk shop."

"I don't think Mr Featherstone would like to hear you call his emporium a junk shop. Antiques, he says they are."

"Antiques, my eye. He recognises a mug when he sees one. He gets them tins in 'specially for Uncle Jim. He's a rip off merchant." Warming to her theme, "You mark my words when Uncle Jim goes to sell his so-called treasures he'll find he's bought dear to sell cheap."

"You're very cynical this morning, Madam."

"Oo, posh words for a Monday." Linda replaced the tin lid tightly, hoping it would rust shut before she had to use it again. "All I'm saying is that Featherstone - and I don't believe that really is his name; he looks more like a Brown to me – knows that our Jimmy is so determined to have every cocoa tin that was ever made that he'll pay anything to get it."

"What about the ones he picks up in car-boot sales then?" Bet beamed in self-congratulation. "You can't say that he doesn't get a bargain there."

"If the dealers don't get there first. Where do you think Featherstone gets his wares from, eh?"

"You're impossible."

"A genuine bargain from one of those sales is as rare as hens' teeth. Most of them that are left, after the experts have done their dawn raid, are all rusty and not worth fifty p. He might just as well put his money on the gee-gees. He'd have about as much chance of coming out on top."

Bet put her knuckles firmly on her hips, "You know he doesn't approve of gambling."

"What he's doing is no different, to my mind. And they're another bunch that always look at things through rose-tinted glasses. Have you noticed as how they always know how much they've won, but can never remember their losses?" Satisfied that she had made her point and yet determined to ram it home, "Junk collectors are no different."

Gaining momentum Linda continued, "They are no better than estate agents. You go and see any dealer and ask him to value any old bit of junk and I can tell you exactly what you'll get told: 'It's not a good time, for … whatever you want to get rid of.' 'You should have come and seen me last year.' A bunch of crooks the lot of them."

"I don't agree." Bet pulled herself up to her full five foot three. "I think they provide a good service."

"Good service! Good service, my eye! They are just a money-grabbing bunch of parasites. I ask you, have you ever seen a poor junk dealer? Have you?"

The yellow duster fluttered like a flag in a fit.

Bet racked her brains for an answer. "That's just because they've studied and know what's what."

"Rubbish. Oh, they know what's what all right; I'll give you that. They know their junk from the genuine article, I'm sure. But more importantly, they know people. They eat suckers like Uncle Jim for breakfast."

By now Bet was struggling to defend her baby brother's rather bizarre craving. "Jim has a big book. He looks them up in it. He knows what their selling price is."

"Ha! Don't you believe all that codswallop? Them prices are only paid out on undamaged goods. The slightest sign of rust and the price drops through the floor. I'll lay a fiver on a penny that if Uncle Jim tried to sell his tins tomorrow they'd find some excuse not to pay him anything like what he paid for them." Adopting a sarcastic tone, " 'They need to be in an immaculate condition, Mr Smith, to get anything like the price you're asking. No, I'm afraid they are worth a lot less than you think.' "

Wagging her finger at her mother, "They are patronising gits. And don't tell me the shop has to make a profit. I ain't green just 'cos I'm cabbage looking. I bet he don't get half of what he paid."

Bet was beginning to think that her now well-heated daughter had a point. Desperately she tried to dig out a plausible comment from her, by now, well-befuddled head.

"Of course Jim will make a profit, he only paid a few old pence for his tins when he was a kid."

"Don't make me laugh. You spent half your life telling me how little money you and Dad had to manage on. How much did Dad earn in them days? Two quid a week including overtime. You can't keep harping on about how much you could buy with a penny in them days one minute and try convincing me that Jimmy's tins cost him nothing the next. I bet he had to save up for weeks to get enough money to buy his blooming tins."

"Some of them were free. He started collecting ones that my Mum got from the grocers."

"And I bet he nagged her to buy a different make or size every week just so that he could have the empties."

She was not going to give in. Bet could see that; she'd go to hell and back on a donkey before she'd give in.

At last Bet had an iron tight case. "What about tax?"

"What tax? VAT?"

"No, stupid! Income tax. I heard a lot of people collect things like oil paintings and the like to avoid paying tax."

Linda nearly split her sides with laughter. Trying to control herself she put her hand over her mouth to stop her teeth falling out.

"Mum, you really are the giddy limit. Tax? Income tax?

When did Uncle Jim ever pay income tax? They don't pay income tax on the social."

"But he's worked all his life." Bet was determined to defend her brother to the end.

"That's as may be. I shouldn't broadcast that around the streets if I was you."

Beverley tapped on the window before entering. She hugged her mother and sister. "You two arguing again, I could hear you from the street."

Linda put her arm around her mother's shoulder. "You look after your old table with beeswax, if you want to."

Beverley went to put her basket on the table.

"Don't put that thing on my table. You'll scratch it."

"Don't worry, Mum, only teasing. And don't worry about your little brother. He's as cunning as a fox. He'll be alright in his old age."

"What are you talking about? There is nothing underhand about your uncle, my girl. Straight as a die he is and always has been."

Beverley sided with her sister, "He's a crafty blighter, that's what he is."

"Don't you start, Beverley. You treat your elders with more respect. He fought in the war for the likes of you two."

"So he might have done and I'm sure we are all grateful, but I'm telling you he's done alright for himself. He'll be a burden to no-one."

"I think you'd better explain yourself." Bet was really getting her dander up.

Beverley grinned. "My darling, crafty uncle has been saving those rusty old tins for donkey's years so he can sell them in his old age for a fortune."

"Isn't that exactly what I've been trying to tell Linda, for the last I don't know how long."

"That's what he wants everyone to think."

"This is all getting far too complicated for me." Bet wiped her hand across her brow and sat down heavily. "I think I need a cuppa."

"You'll get your tea in a minute. Hear me out." Bev sat down opposite her mother. "Uncle Jim has been saving all the money he got from moonlighting over the years in old socks. His mattress is stuffed with notes."

"Poppycock! He hasn't got a bank account."

Bev despaired of ever getting her stubborn mother to listen. "Precisely. If he had a bank account the tax people would have rumbled him years ago. He's got to sell his wretched tins and pretend to get a fortune to cover his tracks."

Linda was flabbergasted. "What! When I think of what my old man gets taken out of his hard-earned money, drained by PAYE it is. The crafty old beggar. You wait 'til I get my hands on him, I'll give him a piece of my mind."

"And what about your part-time jobs, sister darling? When did you last declare all of them? People in glass houses ... what about the mote in your own eye: bible you know?"

"Stop it you two. I'll not have religion in this house." Bet rose, taking the kettle to the cold-water tap at her old stone sink. She'd have to work out the rights and wrongs of it later. "Well I never. I think it's time we all sat down for a nice cup of tea."

End

# NUMBER'S UP

by

Joan Stanley

"Whoever would have thought I'd end up living in a graveyard with a lot of has-beens like you and at the side of a noisy railway line: the Victoria line, at that. So many in one place, packed in like scarlet sardines. I don't know what they're thinking about. It's all right for you. I don't know how I shall bear it. It's so humiliating, so undignified, so degrading; whoever would have thought that it would have come to this? When I remember, have I told you about…?"

"Oh, shut up, Dolly, of course we've heard about it a thousand times. You do go on. It's no good rabbiting on about the past."

"Dorothea to you, if you don't mind."

"Hoity-toity! It's not that bad here, there's a lot of us here from all over these parts. We have a good old chinwag at times, comparing notes, you might say, catching up with the latest gossip from the new boxes when they come in. We used to have a lot of people talking *in* us they never talked *to* us. We could never join in or pass an opinion. I must say you really caused a stir when you arrived. You really must learn to accept reality or you'll make yourself ill and your paint'll drop off."

"It's not so bad for you. By the look of you, you had rust patches long before you got here."

"That's old age. It don't matter where you come from when rust sets in you've got to accept you're past your prime."

"No, Maisie, that's not true. I had a good rub down and makeover every year or so. I always looked as fresh as paint."

"No doubt. It was debatable who wore most paint you or your customers."

"So common! Clients, dear, clients."

"Whatever. You call 'em what you want. It's all the same to me."

"You can hardly put the rich and famous in the same category as the riff-raff that used your facilities."

"Suppose so. But don't you see that's why you was made redundant at such a young age. Your lot was the first to get mobile phones. You just weren't needed any more."

"You do enjoy hurting my feelings, don't you? I'm glad you recognise that I'm a lot younger than you. Well - you could hardly miss it. I am in much better condition than you ever were."

"I might be old and rusty, but at least I was wanted for a lot longer than you were."

"You bitch!"

"Very ladylike, I'm sure."

"No one could ever use the word to describe you. Look at you, all covered in graffiti and telephone numbers. I dread to think what they're advertising. Look at your money receptacle. It's in a dreadful state."

"Tell me about it! It's hell when they prise your cash box open. And for what? A few measly ten-p's."

"I thought, by the way you spoke, you'd have had a lot of cash in you. Not as popular as we made out, then?"

"You'd be surprised what I was used for and it had nothing to do with making calls. Ah, me! I've seen some sights in my time. Did I tell you about the couple that squeezed themselves in one wet night? Cor! They really did…"

"Oh, please, spare me the details. Isn't it enough that I have to endure this place with all of you?"

"They only want glass boxes these days. You can't have a cuddle in one of them; they ain't got no doors. They say our bright red paint sticks out too much: offends the eye."

"I thought that was the point – to get us noticed."

"There you are. That's people for you, don't know what they want."

"I wonder what will happen to us. "

"You worry too much. People are such funny unpredictable creatures. You wait and see. We'll outlive the lot of 'em. I'll put money on it, we'll be bought up by some cranky junk dealers who'll sell us for a fortune to some rich Americans."

"Yes, you're right. I will definitely be spotted by an antiques expert and end up in a mansion or hotel. You never know it might even belong to one of my old customers."

"I thought you only had clients."

"It's this place. It's having an effect on me. You lot are dragging me down to your level."

"You're one of us now, whether you like it or not. We none of us know how long it's going to be before someone pushes our buttons again."

"That's true. You might be common, Maisie, but you're a good friend."

"I must admit I miss the excitement of the 999s and the lovey-dovey calls."

"I didn't hear a lot of that. Most of mine were men making excuses to the little woman for being late at the office."

"That's a laugh. If they was at the office they wouldn't need you."

"You're probably right. You know I never thought of that before ... Do you think there's any danger of us getting scrapped?"

"No, not you. You're well maintained. Don't worry you'll

get bought up and end up somewhere real posh."

"What about you, Maisie?"

"Don't worry about me, luv, I'm determined to be the next Tardis. I've always had a soft spot for Dr Who."

"Now who's living in cuckoo land?"

"I know – but a girl's got a right to dream, ain't she?"

End

# FUN IN MY LITTLE SHOP

by

Joan Stanley

Me? Bingo? No, not me. I work every evening except Sundays; church day, Sunday is. No offence, but Bingo's gambling, it ain't right.

It's a long old day in my little shop, six in the morning to ten at night. Well it's OK really. There's not much on telly these days, is there?

You get your regulars, you know. Some of them come in three or four times a day. I wonder if they've got homes to go to. Lonely, I suppose. Others can't bear to be out of my little shop, in case they miss a bit of gossip.

We have some fun, sometimes. Like when Edna and I chased those sticky fingered kids. Took a handful of penny sweets each, they did. As I've said, my name's not Twiggy, but our Edna could give me a few stone.

She and I chased them kids down the road. We might be fat, but we're still surprisingly fast. We weren't going to let 'em get away with nicking our profits. They ran to the end of the street and stopped. You should have seen their faces, when they looked round and saw us two, right behind them.

I nearly couldn't run; I was splitting myself. Lor', I did laugh.

We grabbed 'em and took 'em back to the shop. And locked 'em in the storeroom and called the police. They were really glad to see the boys in blue. It turned out they were more frightened of Edna and me than the coppers.

Edna's a bit of a caution. She does a bit of cleaning for us. I remember when our lad wouldn't get out of bed for school. He gave her a bit of lip. She ordered him out of bed. He wouldn't get up. She threatened to bounce on him if he didn't move. He wouldn't. She did. She actually took a flying leap and landed - not on him, because he saw her coming and rolled out onto the floor - on the bed. That bed was never the same again.

My husband used to do the newspapers, and get the boys organised, before he went to work.

Nick and I used to do a milk round. It wasn't very big. We had a carrycot on wheels that my daughter'd had as a doll's pram. It wasn't a doll's pram. It was for a proper baby. Do you know it was cheaper than a doll's pram? And, I thought, it must last longer because it was tested to take a baby and you can't have babies falling out of carrycots, all over the place, can you? Those doll's prams cost more and are really flimsy things. Well, I was not wrong. We used the wheels to put the crates of milk on and the cot got used for her first baby.

It was all right, to start with. We only took one crate of twenty out per street. Two or three trips and we were finished. But as the round grew, the poor old wheels struggled. And then one day it died on us, right in the middle of the road.

We used the car after that. It wasn't so good. You had to keep getting in and out. And had to find parking spaces. We did well on the milk round. Good for business, too, because people had to come into the shop and pay their bills. They never got out without buying something, I saw to that.

That milk round nearly got my husband a punch on the nose. One day, I was sitting on the till. No. Not on the till, on its shelf. And a dirty great bloke came in the shop. Stood in front of me and rolled his sleeves up.

"Who, here, has the milk round?" he spluttered.

I think he'd had a few - for Dutch courage.

"Where's the … (I won't say what he said) who's on my patch? You've nicked my trade, with your cheap milk, and I can't make enough out of these roads anymore."

He looked all round the shop.

"Where is he? I'll knock his (mm mm) head off."

"What do you mean? "Where's he?" " I was enjoying this

bit. I could see what he was on. He didn't look capable of hitting a woman, so I strung him along.

"The bloke what delivers the milk."

"That's me and my kid," I said.

"What. But you're a (mm mm) woman."

I looked at him, old fashioned. He got very het up.

"Well, think yourself very lucky you're not a man," he said and stormed out of the shop.

It's the first time I did think it was good *not* to be a man. What I says is this: there will never be equality, until men have babies.

What did you say? Is that the time? Oh, never mind. I've got a Housey-Housey game somewhere. It's better than your Bingo. You match up pictures, not boring old numbers. But I suppose it's the prizes you go for, i'n't it?

Now, now, don't fret yourself so. There'll be another bus along in half an hour. You'll still be in time for the second half. We'll have a nice cup of tea while you're waiting and I'll tell you all about ...

If you're sure, I suppose a walk would do you good."

End

# FOOTPRINTS in the CORNFLAKES

by

Joan Stanley

"Hurry up, Jim. You've got half an hour to get out of the door or you'll be late for school."

"Don't panic, Mum, I've got loads of time."

"No you haven't. You still haven't finished your homework." Maggie peered over his shoulder at the scrawl he euphemistically called handwriting. "You've nowhere near finished; I can only see a title."

Jim instinctively covered his work with his hands, but his reactions were too slow for his eagle-eyed mother.

" 'Footprints In The Cornflakes' by Ivor Wheatear. What kind of title is that?"

"I like it. I thought I'd write about aliens."

"Hmm. Why kids can't live in the real world, I don't know."

"Perhaps they are in the real world ... "

"Don't start that again. I've no time for your nonsense."

Maggie fussed about in her immaculate kitchen; she did not understand why she felt so nervous. At all costs she mustn't let Jim see she was in a dither. She went into the garden and picked some daffodils for the lounge, anything to take her mind off Rupert. But it was futile; she was an emotional mess, both longing for, and dreading, the morning to come.

Jim closed his exercise book and reached for his blazer.

"Now what're you doing? You haven't finished your homework."

"And whose fault is that? I'll just explain to the teacher that you spent so much time arguing about my title that I didn't have time to write it up."

Kids! They always succeed in putting their parents in the wrong. Maggie turned on her heel and stormed out of the kitchen. "I was going to offer you a lift to school, but now I won't have time."

Jim cursed as he wandered down the garden path. He'd definitely scored an own goal this time.

Maggie put the kettle on for the inevitable cup of tea. She hated having arguments with Jim. He was growing up fast and, since his father's death, definitely considered himself to be the man of the house. How on earth was she going to tell him she had met someone who she hoped would become very special to her?

She found it difficult to believe she could ever find anyone to take Steve's place. But here she was feeling weak at the knees just thinking of meeting Rupert for coffee this morning.

The boiling kettle forgotten, Maggie started to clear away the breakfast things. Her mind was anywhere but in her kitchen. Marmalade on the top shelf, sugar underneath, dirty crockery in the dishwasher; her robotic movements performed with no conscious effort from herself.

A whooshing noise brought her to her senses. Maggie tried in vain to catch the box; she only succeeded in aiding gravity to scatter the golden flakes still further. She stared with unbelieving eyes at the cereal on her kitchen floor.

A sob rose in her throat. "Oh, not today. Please, not today. I don't have time to clear up this mess and get ready to go out."

Maggie wanted to look her best without it being obvious that she'd made any effort and that effect could not be achieved in five minutes.

She shut the kitchen door behind her; it was easier to blot out the image of domestic chaos when it was out of sight. Maggie was glad that time was running out; she had never felt so flustered since she was a teenager.

Rupert took her elbow and guided her through the crowd; it was good to feel protected. Normally, she was the tower of strength and everyone leaned on her for support.

"Where are we going? I thought we were going to the coffee shop." Tripping down the village High Street in her rarely worn high heels she was conscious of every cobblestone in the pavement.

"Not today. We are going somewhere quieter where we can talk in comfort and get to know each other better."

No 'by your leave', Maggie thought. She was not used to being taken over in this way. She didn't know if she liked being bossed about. And yet, he was not giving orders; there was nothing offensive in his manner.

He steered her towards an hotel entrance.

"We can't eat here. We'll need a mortgage." She tried to remember how much money she had brought with her and at the same time work out what she needed for the rest of the week.

"My treat."

"No, we should go Dutch."

"I won't hear of it. You don't know what a pleasure it is for me to be able to spend time with you."

Maggie was not sure if she could cope with all this old-world charm. She had always been brought up to distrust smarmy characters. Her Steve had been a very straight-forward guy; he would not have wasted his money on posh décor. And Rupert! What a name! What had his parents been thinking of? Jim will fall about laughing when he hears it; he'll never take him seriously. Maggie groaned to herself, anticipating all the puerile Rupert Bear jokes that her son's fertile imagination would conjure up. And he'll have a field day with the posh accent. How on earth did she get involved with someone like this?

They shared their life histories over a large pot of coffee and a plate of Danish pastries. Maggie licked the sugar off her fingers. "I'll have to eat salad for a week after this lot."

"You'd look pretty whatever …"

"Look, Rupert, if we are to get along you've got to stop putting me on a pedestal." Maggie decided that she must take the bull by the horns. "Are you free for lunch? I'd like you to have a bite to eat with Jim and me at home and, please, stop complimenting me all the time, I'm not used to it. - The longer I leave it the more upset he will be."

"Are you ashamed of me? I don't bite."

"No, no, of course not. It's just that Jim can be very possessive." She hesitated, "And to be honest you are so different from his Dad."

"If it's what you'd like, I'd be delighted."

"And, Rupert, please, relax. You always seem to be on your best behaviour."

"I didn't realise. It's sort of ingrained; I was sent to school when I was five and my parents were very strict."

"I must warn you, Jim is not as well-mannered as I'd like.

He's bound to poke fun at your name."

"Oh, don't worry about that. He can't come up with anything worse than I had to put up with at Prep." He laughed at the quizzical look on Maggie's face. "School, to you."

Maggie turned the key in the front door and leant on it hard. It did not budge. "I'm sorry, Rupert. It won't open, you know what these cottages are like, the slightest damp and..." She shrugged her shoulders and blushed to her roots.

"I know; you always use the back door." Putting his arm around her waist, "Maggie, it's your total lack of falseness which impresses me. Please, just be you. I know I'm going to love your little palace."

Maggie relaxed. She was proud of her well-kept home, even if she had nothing of any great value in it. She liked to be house-proud.

Leading the way to the back of the cottage she opened the door, which was never locked, and walked straight in.

"You can't go in." Maggie turned sharply, pushing Rupert out of the doorway as she pulled the door behind her. "It ... You ... I ..."

"What on earth's the matter?"

Maggie burst into tears. "I'm so ashamed. I left the

kitchen in an awful mess this morning. You see Jim and I had a few words and I upset the cornflakes and …"

"You're not making any sense. Whatever needs doing we'll sort out together." Rupert hesitated, "That is if you want me to. I do not mean to intrude."

Maggie smiled at his lost boy expression, glad to find some relief from the tension building up inside her.

"What did you argue about, if I'm allowed to ask?"

"It was nothing really. Jim was writing a story for school and he gave it a silly title. He needs to take his work more seriously."

Rupert opened the door and let himself in. "I see what you mean."

Maggie stared at the floor. 'Footprints In The Cornflakes'; it was quite good, really. Why did she make such a fuss and get upset. She intended to apologise to Jim when she saw him.

"There *are* footprints in the cornflakes." She stepped back into the arms of a very surprised Rupert. "Look."

"Eh? I must say you are a girl for the unexpected."

"I did not tread on them, I swear I didn't."

"Well, if you didn't who did?" Putting her to one side, "If you don't mind I think I should take a look around," pulling himself up to his full six foot two. "You stay here."

"Be careful."

Maggie was used to sorting out her own problems, but this time she was pleased to let Rupert have his own way.


"What the hell is going on in here?" Jim threw open the back door and scrunched his way across the kitchen floor. "Where's my lunch? You know I don't have long. You always have it ready."

"I brought a friend home."

"You what? Why are the cornflakes on the floor?"

"I spilt them, before I went out."

"And you didn't clear them up? Where have you been?"

"Hang on a minute, this is getting out of hand. Who do you think you're talking to?"

It sounded as though pandemonium had broken out upstairs.

"Did you hear that? Do you know who's up there?"

"It's Rupert. He's looking around."

"Rupert who? Bear?"

"Don't start."

"Since when have you been entertaining men in your bedroom while I've been at school?"

"How dare you. You …"

"It's alright. I get the picture. I thought you were different. I'll be glad when I'm old enough to leave home."

"Never mind all that. What is going on? He only went to look because I saw footprints in the cornflakes."

Coming to the conclusion that his mother was losing it in more ways than one, Jim took the stairs two at a time and entered his mother's room to find two men locked in a wrestling hold.

"Ring the police," Rupert ordered.

"Who are you?"

"Not now, Jim, get the bloody police."

Maggie giggled. She didn't think Rupert was capable of such vulgarity. Then she was overcome with anger. Her nightclothes and most intimate possessions were strewn over the bed.

Without thought of the consequences she grabbed a heavy stone vase from the window sill and raised her arm to strike, "Oh no, you have no right to touch my things. You're a dirty pervert."

"I was only looking for your jewellery, Missus, you'd be amazed where people hide their stuff."

"You'll have to bring it in this house before you can take it out."

Taking advantage of the moment, Rupert felled the intruder with a well-practised rugby tackle and bundled him into the wardrobe. He shoved the bed against the door, "That'll hold him for a bit."

Jim was impressed. "OK, Mum. You win. You are clearly not safe to be left alone and I can't be here to keep you out of trouble all the time.

Maggie cuffed the air above his head.

"Mind my hair."

"You'll do. Rupert meet Jim.

The two men in her life shook hands.

"It's on condition, you understand, that you don't come round here in your yellow check trousers and red jumper.

End

# A STATIONARY TALE

by

Joan Stanley

"Come on. If you don't hurry up we'll miss the train." Stella urged the twins to run across the bridge to platform four. "Don't run down the stairs, you'll fall over."

"Make up your mind, Mum." Brenda sounded fed up already and the day had just begun.

"It's not going to help if you trip over and break your necks, is it?"

"We're alright, you watch yourself. You're not as young as you used to be. You're puffing like an old steam engine."

"If you two carried some of these cases I could get along faster."

Bradley looked back at his struggling mother, "But then we'd get behind and you'd nag us for holding you up, Mum."

"Kids!"

Arriving on the platform with five minutes to spare, Stella heaved the bags onto a bench and flopped down beside them. The twins rushed to the newsstand to buy a couple of comics and returned with their noses well buried in the latest exploits of Dennis the Menace and Desperate Dan.

"Why the rush, Mum. We've got here in plenty of time. There's no sign of the train."

"It's better to be early than late. You can always waste a few minutes, but if you're late ..."

"It's always the same. You always panic, and for what? It's going to be boring. It always is. I'd be happy not to go at all."

"Me, too."

"Tough. It's important to visit your Great-aunt Gertie. She looks forward to our visits. She old and lonely; can't get about much these days."

"The old girl can get about when she wants to. Never misses Bingo, from what I hear."

"Watch your mouth, Brad. You'll be old yourself one day."

Always ready to support her brother, Brenda agreed. "She's having you on, Mum. It's just that you can't see it."

"Maybe. I quite like to see the old biddy. Talk about old times." Stella stared across the track at nothing in particular; she was already looking forward to sharing the latest bit of family gossip with her aunt. Anticipating the 'No's' and 'Never's' she'd get in reply.

"Look, Brad, there's a new Dennis t-shirt on sale."

The twins looked up at their mother to see what her response would be to this vital piece of information.

Her response instinctive: "No, you can't have one."

Stella could be stubborn at times. The look on her face told Brad that this was not the time to argue. "Who said I wanted one anyway?"

*"We are sorry to announce that the 9.15 to Victoria has been delayed. It will be approximately 15 minutes late."*

"Oh, no. Not another quarter of an hour. Let's go home, Mum."

"Yes, Mum," Bradley agreed, "It's freezing out here. We'll catch our death."

Stella started to collect the bags together. "For goodness sake, stop moaning. We'll go into the waiting room. It'll be warmer in there."

"Fantastic. Grab that bag, Bren, give Mum a hand. I'll take the heavy one, Mum. Can we have a choc-ice from the shop?"

"I'll have a strawberry lolly."

"Cupboard lovers! I thought you two were just complaining about the cold."

"But it's warmer in here, just like you said it would be, Mum."

"Hmm." Stella smiled as the glow of the coal fire warmed her cheeks.

"Can I have another comic, Mum? I've read this one."

"Me, too."

"No, you can't. Patience is all you two need."

"I'm fed up. We've been here well over half an hour."

"It can't be much longer. You'll see." Stella wouldn't admit it to the twins, but, if it wasn't for her determination not to give in to her demanding offspring, she would have dearly loved to give up the excursion and head back home for a nice cup of tea, in front of her own fire, and a bit of telly.

*"We are sorry to announce that the 9.15 to Victoria has been cancelled due to a car getting stuck on a level crossing. The next train to Victoria is due to arrive in half an hour. We are sorry for any inconvenience caused to our passengers."*

"That's it. We're going home. I'm not sitting here for another half an hour." Adjusting her headscarf and putting her gloves back on, Stella stood up to leave.

"Good ol' Mum." The twins collected their comics and stuffed them into their pockets.

*"Hello, Bert, what are you doing up here. Ain't you got no work to do on the station?"*

*"Nah. Me broom's got fed up with me leaning on it all day."*

*"You are awful, Bert. What would the stationmaster say if he could hear you talk like that?"*

*"But he can't, can he."* Bert sniffed. *"I had a narrow escape this*

*morning. Some old bag turned up with two scruffy kids and a pile of*
*bags. I scarpered a bit quick, in case she thought I was going to help*
*her with 'em."*

*"Naughty boy. You'll get the sack one day, you will."*

*"Not as naughty as I'd like to be." ·*

*"No, Bert. Not in here, Bert. Someone might come in."*

*"You know as well as I do that no-one ever comes up here. Got a*
*good view of the station, I must say. I didn't realise you could see so*
*much from your little cubbyhole. There's a good view in here, too,*
*Millie."*

*"What are you looking at …? Get your hands off."*

*"I was just trying to improve the view a bit more."*


"Hear that, Bren?" Brad poked his sister in the ribs with his
elbow. "I wonder what he's got in mind." ·

"It don't need much imagination to work that one out,
does it?" The children sniggered together.

"Come on, you two, less of that," Stella reprimanded, but
they noticed that she didn't seem in any hurry to collect her
bags and leave. She sat down again on the bench outside the
waiting room. "Perhaps we'll wait a bit longer. Aunt
Gertrude would be very disappointed if we let her down.
You know how much she looks forward to our visits."

"But it's cold out here. If we do have to wait, why can't
we wait inside?"

"We can hear the announcements better out here. Just settle down and wait."

"It couldn't be anything to do with the entertainment, could it, Mum?"

"I don't know what you mean."


*"Bert Budgen, what the hell are you doing up here. Get your backside back on the platform or I'll ..."*

*"Ok, ok, hold you hair on, Boss. I bet you were as bad when you were young, if you can remember that far back."*

*"Enough of your cheek, get your arse down those stairs and find some work to do."*

A female giggle followed the command. *"What, and break the habit of a lifetime?"*

*"Don't you encourage him, young Millie. He's lazy enough without your help."*

*"But at least he's good looking with it, Mr Grainger. But not in the distinguished way you are, of course."*

*"There you are, boss, begging for attention she is."*

*"Get out of here, before I loose my rag."*

*"It is getting a bit crowded up here, I'll see you later, Doll."*

*"Go on, go on, before I help you down those stairs with my boot."*

*"I'm going, I'm going."*

*"And turn that damned tannoy off, Millie. The whole station could hear everything you two were up to."*

"That's nice for 'em."

"BERT!"

"I'm gone."

"What a shame, Mum, it was just getting interesting. I suppose she'll turn it off now."

"It's ..."

"It's not nice listening in to other people's affairs," Brenda mimicked the reply she anticipated her mother would have given.

"Affairs about the right word, if you ask me."

This side of the station was beginning to get a bit crowded as people stood around wondering if the London train would ever turn up. Several waiting passengers were seen to be talking to each other as hushed conversations were breaking out up and down the platform.

"I'm sorry about all that, Millie. A nice young lady like you doesn't want to be associating with riff-raff like Bert. He'll never get anywhere in this life."

"Mum. She didn't turn the thing off, after all."

"It's none of your business. Be quiet, can't you."

"So she can hear better, Brad, that's what she means."

"Don't be disgusting."

"He's not all that bad, Mr Grainger. He's a rough diamond, you might say. Got a heart as big as a bucket."

"But what can he offer a young lady like you, Millie? He earns next to nothing, whereas I have a decent salary and a large car. And I'd take you on holiday abroad every year, Millie. Just the two of us, basking in the sun. What does that sound like?"

"Sounds lovely, Mr Grainger. I love the sun."

"And I bet you look gorgeous in a bikini. Think of the tan you'd get. Oh, please call me Godfrey. No need to stand on ceremony with me."

"Well … Godfrey … I don't think Bert would like it."

"Forget Bert. You deserve far better. Think of all the nice things I can buy you. What have you got now, a bed-sit in Railway Terrace? I'd even be prepared to set you up in your own flat … if we got especially friendly."

"I say. How about I think about it and let you know?"

"And while you're about it you can think about his wife and three kids, Millie."

"Bert!"

"I thought I told you to get back to work, Budgen."

"So I did. And a good job, too. That tannoy sounds really good from the platform."

"What?"

"You should have made sure she turned that thing off, like you told her to, Grainger, before you started your anky-panky."

"Don't you dare call me by my surname. You're fired!"

"I don't think so, Sir. You see I've phoned the Gov'ner and he's on

86

*his way. She's my girl and I'm not letting you try your wicked ways on my innocent little Millie."*

*"Innocent, my eye!"*

*"Don't you think you've said enough for one morning, Boss?"*

*"I haven't finished with you yet."*

"Look, Bren, there's another bloke trying to get in. Looks more crowded up there than it does down here on the platform."

*"Mr Grainger, I would like a word with you in your office, if you don't mind. And turn that blasted loud speaker off, girl."*

*"I can't, Sir, the Victoria train is just arriving at platform four."*

*"Get the wretched thing announced and come downstairs immediately."*

*"What about the next train. It will be here in a few minutes."*

*"Blast the bloody trains!"*

*"The train now arriving on platform four is the 9.45 for Victoria, passengers for …"*

"Come on Brenda, move yourself or we'll never get a seat. Grab a bag, Brad, there's a good lad."

*"… should change at …"*

"We'll really have something to tell Aunt Gertie when we get to London, Mum."

"Who said only women gossip?"

End

# GETTING DOWN TO IT IN MY LITTLE SHOP

by

Joan Stanley

Take cigarettes. So far as I'm concerned you can take 'em as far as you like. I don't know why I sell fags at all. There's no money in it. Tax. Most of what people pays for 'em is tax.

Why shouldn't I have a moan if I want to? Shopkeeping's not what it was.

Glorified tax collectors. That's what we are. Typical. The government even manages to tax people for the pleasure of giving themselves bronchitis. Not that I ever liked the filthy things, made me sick, they did.

I do wish people didn't smoke. Funny things, cigarette packets. You can stack up so many and then - they all fall down. You know there's room on the shelf for one more, but can you get the last one to stay up? - No. And when one row collapses, down they all go. Just like dominoes.

I wouldn't mind, but they fall under the shelf with the till on it. It's very narrow where our till is and I'm not as thin as I used to be. It's a bit awkward getting down there and darn nigh impossible to get up, again.

With the ciggy packets in your hand, you've got nothing to hold on with, to give yourself a pull up, 'ave you? Well I suppose you wouldn't know, would you?

It's like getting out of the bath. It's all the fault of the bath foam stuff. You know, the stuff that makes you soft and irresistible. Well as I said, I've put on a bit of weight and I nearly break my neck when I try and get out of the bath.

We've just had the bath re-enameled and they say we shouldn't use a bath mat with suckers on, 'cos it will pull the new surface off. I think they should have stuck it on better. What's the point of having a new bath surface, if you don't know when it's going to fall off?

You're not allowed to put the hot water in first, either. Have you noticed, if you put the cold water in first, it makes the bottom of the bath cold? And then my bottom gets cold, when I sit down. It's worse in winter because the water coming out the tap is freezing.

As I was saying, the bubbles make the bath slippery. I was in a right pickle. Funny that - back to the beetroot! Now where was I, oh yes, I was in a terrible state the other Saturday morning. My luxury that, a bath on Saturday morning, while the Saturday girl is in the shop.

It was no good me crying out for help. One thing, nobody would hear me and other thing, I'd locked the door.

Try as I could, whenever I tried to get up, my feet slipped away from me and I ended up sitting down, again.

I was getting really fed up with this, when I worked out that if I lifted myself a couple of inches and wedged one foot under my ... underneath me, and put the other leg out straight, with a heave I got lift off; just like a rocket.

But I didn't get to the moon. Get it? Never mind.

Now where was I? Oh yes, cigarettes. I've got crafty, now. I have my broom handy, so, if I knock 'em all down, I can sweep 'em out into the open and pick 'em up easy.

Better still, I usually "notice" they need filling up when someone else is on the till. I'm intelligent like that.

Always was quick, me.

When I was a young girl, and that wasn't last week, you understand, I took the eleven-plus. Funny that, I wonder why they say we 'take' exams. Makes it sound as though it's supposed to be good for us, like jollop from the Doc.

Daft calling it the eleven-plus, as well. I took mine at nine. Did you know you could take it right up to the age of thirteen? Well, I passed to go to the Grammar School. I did.

And my headmistress, a right old dragon she was, didn't believe it. She actually sent my exam papers back to have 'em checked. I may not be good with words, but I'm real quick with figures.

So off I went to the posh school in the town. Took me half an hour by train, steam in them days, and three-quarters of an hour walk to get there in the morning and same again in the evening to get home. No, not the same, the other way round. We didn't have a car in those days and my ol' Mum never did learn to drive.

The first day I arrived in my new uniform. I'd never had a uniform before. I had a navy-blue skirt ...

Oh, you off then? Have a nice time. Might see you in my little shop sometime.

End